STORYTIME COLLECTION

This book belongs to

Autumn
Publishing

Published in 2020
by Autumn Publishing
Cottage Farm
Sywell
NN6 0BJ
www.igloobooks.com

Autumn is an imprint of Bonnier Books UK

0920 004
6 8 10 11 9 7 5
ISBN 978-1-78810-994-9

Printed and manufactured in China

Disney

THE LION KING

STORYTIME COLLECTION

One very special day, on the plains of the savannah, animals of all shapes and sizes were gathered together to celebrate the birth of King Mufasa and Queen Sarabi's son, Simba.

One day, this little cub would become king.

To mark the birth of his son, Mufasa invited Rafiki, his wise baboon friend, to present Simba to the other animals. Rafiki proudly raised the cub high into the air for the excited crowd to see, but there was one animal who wasn't there.

His name was Scar and he was the king's brother. Scar was angry as the birth of Simba meant he no longer had any chance of becoming king. When Mufasa asked why he wasn't there, Scar just skulked away. "Don't turn your back on me, Scar!" roared Mufasa, angrily.

"Oh no, Mufasa," replied Scar, snarling. "Perhaps you shouldn't turn your back on me!"

Time passed, and Simba grew up to be a playful and curious little cub. One morning, as the sun was just beginning to peek above the horizon, Mufasa took Simba to the top of Pride Rock. "Everything the light touches is our kingdom," said Mufasa. "And one day, the sun will rise with you as the new king."

"This will all be mine?" asked Simba. "What about that shadowy place?"

"That is beyond our borders," replied Mufasa. "You must never go there."

Later that day, Simba went to see Scar. He told his uncle how Mufasa had shown him the whole kingdom. "He didn't show you what's beyond the northern border?" asked Scar.

"Well, no," replied Simba, sadly. "He said I couldn't go there."

"He's absolutely right," said Scar. Knowing Simba would be curious, he added, "An elephant graveyard is no place for a young prince."

Scar made it sound so exciting that Simba knew he had to go. Then he could show his father how brave he was.

Excited to visit the graveyard, but not wanting to go alone, Simba asked his best friend, Nala, to come along. Though Simba had lied to his mother about where they were going, Sarabi still insisted Zazu, the king's servant, went with them. "How are we going to ditch the dodo?" asked Nala. Luckily for the two cubs, Simba already had a plan.

As they were wandering past a herd of zebras, Simba and Nala suddenly darted in between them and, before long, they had escaped Zazu.

But, as the pair reached the graveyard, excitement turned to fear. The old bones cast scary-looking shadows across the ground. Suddenly, three hyenas appeared and moved menacingly towards the two cubs.

Suddenly, Zazu appeared, and placed himself between the hyenas and the two naughty cubs. But the drooling, hungry hyenas kept on coming.

R-R-ROAR! Out of nowhere, Mufasa appeared! He swiped and slammed the hyenas with his giant paws. "Don't ever come near my son again!" he growled, as the three bullies ran away, whimpering.

After telling Zazu to take Nala home, Mufasa turned to face Simba. "I'm very disappointed in you," he said.

"I was just trying to be brave," said Simba.

As they spoke, neither noticed Scar watching them, angry that his plan had failed.

That night, Mufasa and Simba were lying on the grass, gazing up at the twinkling stars. "The great kings of the past look down on us from those stars," explained Mufasa. "So whenever you feel alone, just remember that those kings will always be there to guide you, and so will I."

The following morning, Scar led Simba into a deep valley. "Wait here," said the devious uncle. "Your father has a surprise for you."

Suddenly, a herd of wildebeest, with hyenas snapping at their heels, came thundering down into the valley towards the lion cub. Simba jumped onto a tree just in time, but was struggling to hang on. Just then, Mufasa appeared and raced down into the valley to try and rescue his son. “Hold on!” he cried.

Mufasa snatched Simba just in time and carried him through the dust and trampling hooves. But just as he placed his son safely on a ledge, some wildebeest knocked Mufasa to the ground.

Battered and bruised, the king struggled to climb back up the rock face. As he neared the top, Scar appeared from above. “Help me!” pleaded Mufasa. Scar leaned closer and reached out with his large paws. Suddenly, he dug his claws into his brother’s legs.

“Long live the king,” whispered Scar, before throwing his brother to the ground, where he disappeared beneath the stampeding wildebeests.

Once the dust had settled, Simba jumped back into the valley and ran to his father. He nuzzled him with his nose, but Mufasa didn't move.

"What have you done?" demanded Scar, who had come down from the top of the cliff.

"He tried to save me!" cried Simba, stammering. "It was an accident."

"If it weren't for you," replied Scar, snarling, "he would still be alive."

"What am I gonna do?" asked Simba.

"Run away and never return," replied Scar.

So, heartbroken and scared, Simba fled.

As Simba ran, the hyenas quickly followed after him. They had orders from Scar to kill the cub and chased him until the little lion fell into a thick patch of thorn bushes. Too cowardly to follow, the hyenas called out to Simba. "If you ever come back, we'll kill you!"

That night, back at Pride Rock, Scar told the lionesses the news that both Mufasa and Simba were dead. “It is with a heavy heart that I become your new king,” he announced, as a large group of hyenas appeared from the shadows. “Out of the ashes of this tragedy,” he continued, “we shall greet a new era of peace in which lion and hyena come together.”

The lionesses were too shocked to say anything.

Days passed and, with no water and the heat of the sun beating down upon him, Simba eventually collapsed. As vultures swooped around him, he was rescued by a meerkat, called Timon, and a warthog, called Pumbaa. They took him to a waterhole, where he slowly woke up. "Where ya from?" asked Timon.

"Who cares?" replied Simba. "I can't go back. I did something terrible."

Timon and Pumbaa's happy-go-lucky attitude to life quickly cheered Simba up. Together, they would sing 'Hakuna Matata', which meant 'no worries', as they danced through the jungle and played in the rivers. Soon, all of Simba's cares were behind him.

As time went by, the little cub grew into a strong, young lion.

One night, Simba was watching the stars with his two friends. "Someone once told me the great kings of the past are up there," said Simba, remembering his father's words.

The next day, as Pumbaa was hunting for bugs, he was chased by a lioness and got stuck under a tree. Just as she was about to pounce, Simba appeared and leapt at her. The two fought. It was then Simba realised who she was.

“Nala!” he cried. “It’s me, Simba.”

“Simba? Everyone thought you were dead!” exclaimed Nala. “But you’re alive! And that means you’re the king!”

Nala's arrival reminded Simba how upset he still was about his father's death. He didn't want to be king either. Unsure what to do, Simba went off to be alone.

However, Nala wasn't the only familiar face nearby. As dusk fell, Rafiki appeared and took the lion to a pool. "Look," insisted Rafiki, pointing to the water. Simba stared hard and saw his father's image appear. "His spirit lives in you," explained the baboon.

Suddenly, Mufasa's image appeared in the clouds above. His voice seemed to fill Simba's very soul. "Remember, you are my son and the one true king," said the vision. As quickly as it had appeared, Mufasa's image faded, but Simba now knew what he had to do.

The next morning, as Nala, Timon and Pumbaa looked for their friend, Rafiki appeared. “The king has returned,” he explained.

“He’s gone back to challenge Scar!” cried Nala, happily.

On returning to his old home, Simba couldn't believe the devastation Scar's rule had caused. The lands were bare and dry. Nothing grew and bones lay everywhere.

Eventually, Nala, Timon and Pumbaa caught up with Simba and insisted on helping. Together, the group of friends went to fight Scar and the hyenas.

Meanwhile, at Pride Rock, Sarabi, Simba's mother, confronted Scar over the lack of food. "The herds have moved. There is nothing left," she explained. "We must leave Pride Rock."

"I am the king and I make the rules," replied Scar

"If you were half the king Mufasa was... " began Sarabi.

A furious Scar shouted, "I am ten times the king Mufasa was!" before knocking the former queen to the ground with one swipe of his paw.

At that moment, there was a loud R-R-ROAR! Scar quickly turned around. "Mufasa!" said the frightened lion. "It can't be! You're dead!"

But it wasn't Mufasa. "Simba!" cried Sarabi. "You're alive!" She was so happy to see her son again.

Simba jumped down in front of Scar. "Step down or fight!" cried the young lion.

Scar chose to fight, and ordered his hyenas to attack Simba. But Nala, the other lionesses, as well as Timon and Pumbaa, bravely fought them off.

Scar tried to sneak away, but Simba chased him to the top of Pride Rock. Scar begged Simba to let him live. "What shall I do?" asked the cowardly lion.

"Run," replied Simba. "Run away and never return."

Suddenly, an angry Scar, filled with years of jealous fury, lunged at Simba. But, with one powerful blow, the young lion knocked Scar aside and hurled him off the cliff.

As rain began to fall, Simba stood on top of Pride Rock and roared triumphantly. Below, the joyful cries of the animals could be heard for miles. The rightful king had returned.

As time passed, Simba, just like his father, became a wise and respected king, with Nala as his queen. Under his rule, the herds returned and the grass and trees grew back. Then, one day, just like all those years ago, Rafiki was asked to present a very special little cub to the world. A cub who would one day grow up to rule the kingdom.

THE END

COLLECT THEM ALL!

With 7 more exciting titles to choose from, you'll want to complete your Storytime Collection!

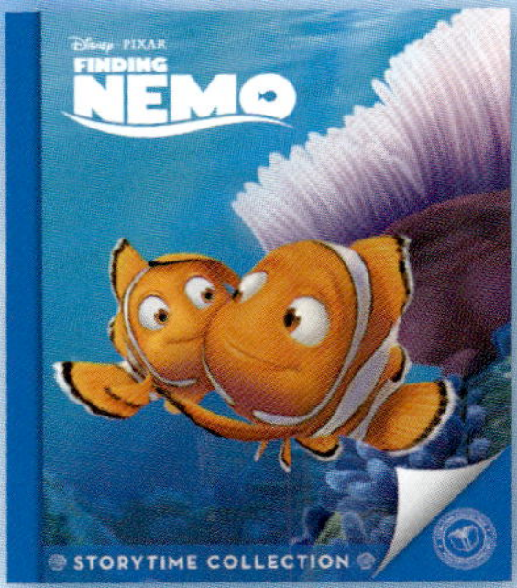

How far will a father go for his son?

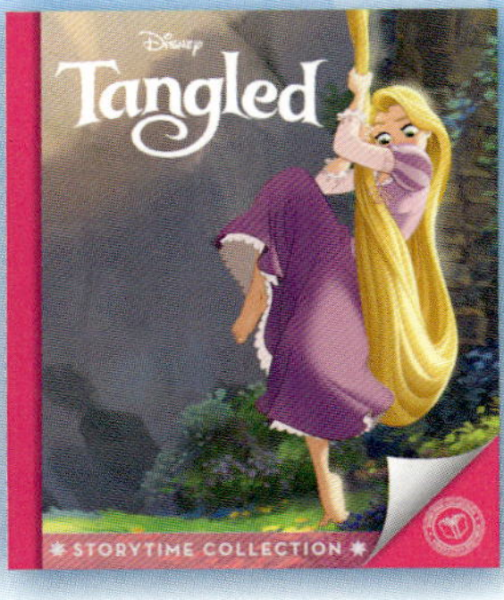

Will Rapunzel learn who she truly is?

Will Moana be able to save the ocean?

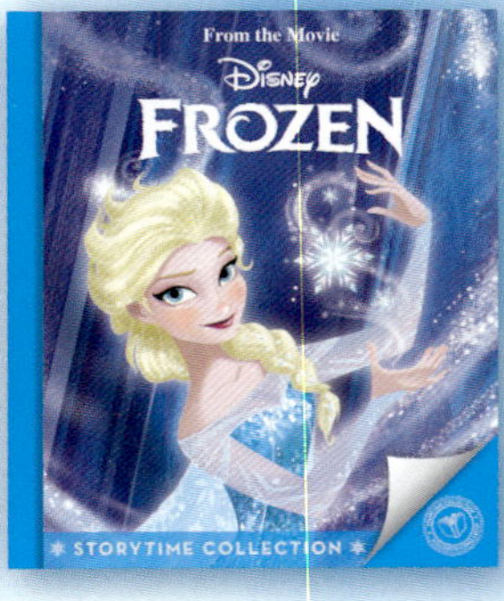

Can Anna and Elsa stop an eternal winter?

Will Mowgli defeat Shere Khan?

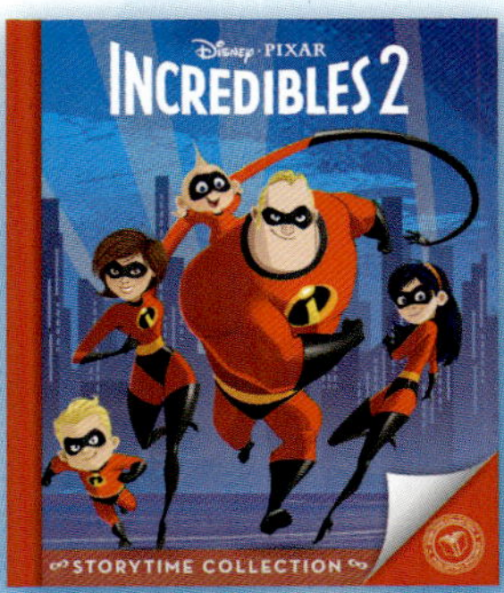

Will the Incredibles save the day?

Will Belle be able to break the curse?